Jack
and the
Beanstalk

*Retold and
illustrated by*

STEVEN KELLOGG

Morrow Junior Books   *New York*

Colored inks, watercolors, and acrylics were
used for the full-color artwork.
The text type is 15 point Clearface.

Library of Congress Cataloging-in-Publication Data
Kellogg, Steven.
Jack and the beanstalk
retold and illustrated by Steven Kellogg.
p.   cm.
Summary: A boy climbs to the top of a giant beanstalk,
where he uses his quick wits to outsmart a giant
and make his and his mother's fortune.
ISBN 0-688-10250-6 (trade).
ISBN 0-688-10251-4 (library)
[1. Fairy tales. 2. Folklore—England.
3. Giants—Folklore.]
PZ8.K366Jac   1991   398.21'0941—dc20
[E]   90-45990   CIP   AC

Author's Note

This book is based on the classic "Jack and the Beanstalk" in *English Fairy Tales*, which was edited by Joseph Jacobs in 1889. He informs us in the Notes and References that "I told this as it was told me in Australia, somewhere about the year 1860." Although this retelling has been adapted for a contemporary picture-book audience, it is faithful to the spirit of Joseph Jacobs's language, retaining some now-remote phrases like "start shop" and words like "peltered" (a synonym for *dashed*) because of their contribution to the character and color of the tale.

Love to our two Sams . . .
princes both

There was, once upon a time, a poor widow who had an only son named Jack and a cow named Milky-white. And all they had to live on was the milk the cow gave every morning, which they carried to the market and sold. But one morning Milky-white gave no milk, and they didn't know what to do.

"Cheer up, Mother. I'll go and get work somewhere,"
said Jack.

"We've tried that before and nobody would take you!"
cried his mother. "We must sell Milky-white and with the
money start shop or something."

On his way to market Jack met a funny-looking old man.
"Well, good morning, Jack," said he.

"Good morning to you," said Jack, and wondered how the
man knew his name.

"Can you tell me how many beans make five?" said the man.

"Two in each hand and one in your mouth," said Jack, sharp
as a needle.

"Right!" said the man. "And as you are such a bright lad, I don't mind doing a swap with you—your cow for these beans."

"Go along," said Jack.

"Ah! But these are magical beans," said the man. "If you plant them tonight, by morning they grow right up to the sky."

"Really?" said Jack.

"Yes, and if it doesn't turn out to be true, you can have your cow back."

"Back already, Jack?" said his mother. "Tell me, how much did you get for Milky-white?"

"You'll never guess, Mother."

"Could it be five pounds...ten...fifteen? No," she cried, "it can't be twenty!"

"I knew you couldn't guess. What do you say to these magical beans? Plant them tonight and—"

"What!" said Jack's mother. "Have you been such a dolt, such an idiot as to give away my Milky-white, the best milker in the parish, for a set of paltry beans? Off with you to bed! And as for your precious beans, here they go out the window."

So Jack went upstairs to his little room in the attic, and sad and sorry he was to be sure, as much for his mother's sake as for the loss of his supper.

At last he dropped off to sleep.

When Jack woke up, he saw that the beans had sprung up into a big beanstalk that went up and up and up till it reached the sky. So the old man spoke the truth, after all.

Jack gave a jump onto the beanstalk, and he climbed and he climbed and he climbed and he climbed and he climbed and he climbed and he climbed till at last he reached the sky.

Jack walked along and he walked along and he walked along till he came to a great big tall house, and on the doorstep was a great big tall woman.

"Good morning, mum," said Jack. "Could you be so kind as to give me some breakfast?"

"It's breakfast you want, is it?" said the great big tall woman. "It's breakfast you'll be if you don't move on. My man is an ogre and there's nothing he likes better than broiled boys on toast."

"Oh, please, mum," cried Jack. "I've had nothing to eat since yesterday morning, really and truly, mum. I may as well be broiled as die of hunger."

Well, the ogre's wife was not half so bad, after all. She took Jack into the kitchen and gave him some bread and cheese, when all of a sudden, thump! Thump! THUMP! The whole house began to tremble with the noise of someone coming.

"Goodness gracious me!" said the ogre's wife. "Come along quick!" And she bundled Jack into the oven just as the ogre came in.

He was a big one, to be sure. "Ah! Wife," he said, "what's this I smell?"

Fee-fi-fo-fum!
I smell the blood of an Englishman.
Be he alive or be he dead,
I'll grind his bones to make my bread.

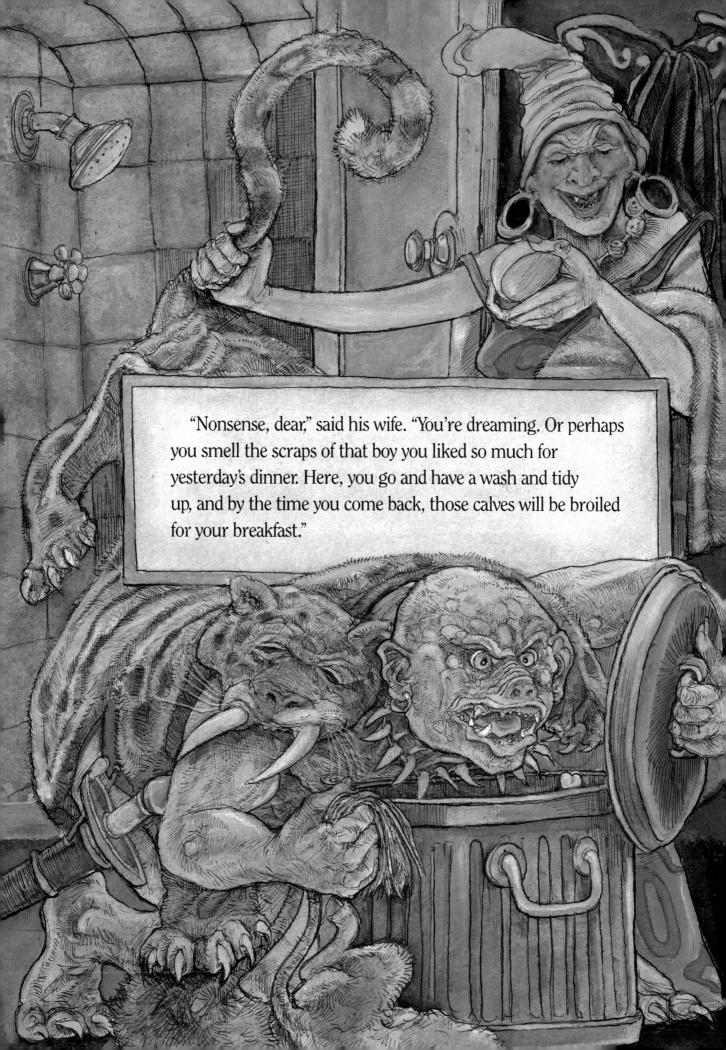

"Nonsense, dear," said his wife. "You're dreaming. Or perhaps you smell the scraps of that boy you liked so much for yesterday's dinner. Here, you go and have a wash and tidy up, and by the time you come back, those calves will be broiled for your breakfast."

Well, the ogre had his breakfast, and after that he went to a big chest and took out a couple of bags of gold, and down he sat and counted. At last his head began to nod and he began to snore till the whole house shook again.

Then Jack crept out of the oven, grabbed a bag of gold, and was off before you could say "Jack Robinson."

When Jack came to the beanstalk, he threw down the gold, which of course fell into his mother's garden.

Then Jack climbed down. "Well, Mother," he said. "Wasn't I right about the beans? They really are magical, you see."

So they lived off the bag of gold for some time, but at last they came to the end of it, and Jack made up his mind to try his luck once more up at the top of the beanstalk.

One fine morning he rose up early and jumped onto the beanstalk, and he climbed and he climbed and he climbed, and he walked and he walked and he walked till at last he came to the great big tall house he had been to before.

There, sure enough, standing on the doorstep was the great big tall woman.

"Go away, my boy," said the big tall woman, "or else my man will eat you up for breakfast. But aren't you the youngster who came here once before? Do you know, that very day my man missed one of his bags of gold."

"That's strange, mum," said Jack, bold as brass. "I daresay I could tell you something about that, but I'm so hungry I can't speak till I've had something to eat."

Well, the big tall woman was so curious that she took him in again.

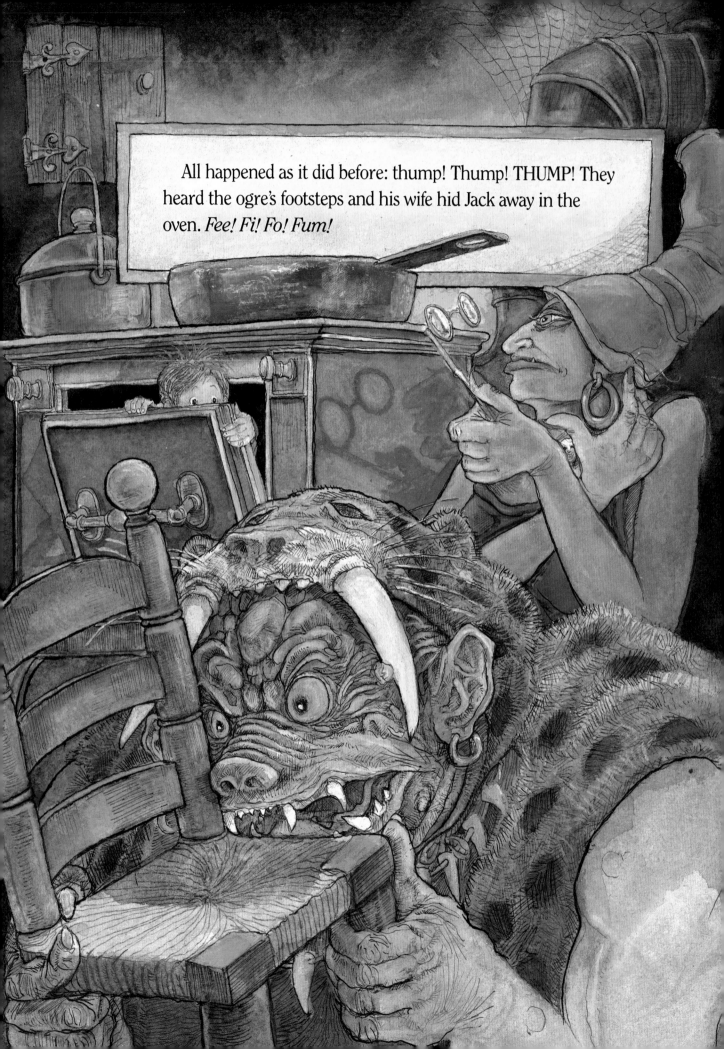

All happened as it did before: thump! Thump! THUMP! They heard the ogre's footsteps and his wife hid Jack away in the oven. *Fee! Fi! Fo! Fum!*

After breakfast the ogre said, "Wife, bring me the hen that lays the golden eggs." So she brought it and the ogre said, "Lay," and it laid an egg all of gold. Soon the ogre began to nod his head and to snore till the house shook. Then Jack tiptoed out of the oven, nabbed the golden hen, and off he peltered.

But this time the hen gave a cackle that woke the ogre, and just as Jack got out of the house, he heard him roaring, "Wife, wife, what have you done with my golden hen?"

When Jack got home, he showed his mother the wonderful hen and said, "Lay" to it, and it laid a golden egg every time he said, "Lay."

Well, it wasn't very long before Jack decided once again to try his luck up there at the top of the beanstalk.

This time he knew better than to go straight to the ogre's house. When the big tall woman came out with a pail, he crept into the house and got into the bread box.

He hadn't been there long when he heard thump! Thump! THUMP! as before, and in came the ogre and his wife. "Fee-fi-fo-fum, I smell the blood of an Englishman. I smell him, wife, I smell him."

"Do you, my dearie?" said the ogre's wife. "Well, if it's the little rogue that stole your gold and the hen, then he's sure to have got into the oven."

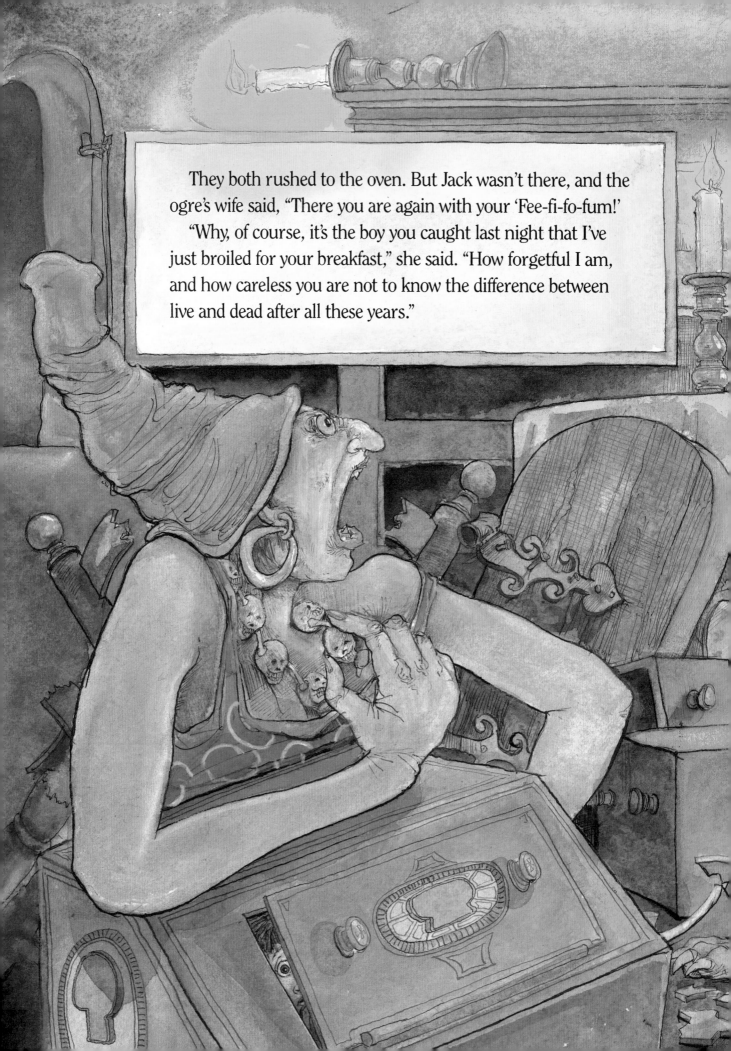

They both rushed to the oven. But Jack wasn't there, and the ogre's wife said, "There you are again with your 'Fee-fi-fo-fum!'"

"Why, of course, it's the boy you caught last night that I've just broiled for your breakfast," she said. "How forgetful I am, and how careless you are not to know the difference between live and dead after all these years."

"Well, I could have sworn..." muttered the ogre, and he searched the larder and the cupboards and everything, only luckily he didn't think of the bread box.

After his breakfast was over, the ogre called out, "Wife, bring me my golden harp." So she brought it and he said, "Sing!" and the golden harp sang most beautifully.

And it went on singing till the ogre fell asleep and began to snore like thunder.

Then Jack lifted the lid very quietly and crept like a mouse on hands and knees till he came to the table and up he crawled and caught hold of the golden harp.

But the harp called out, "Master! Master!" and the ogre
woke up.

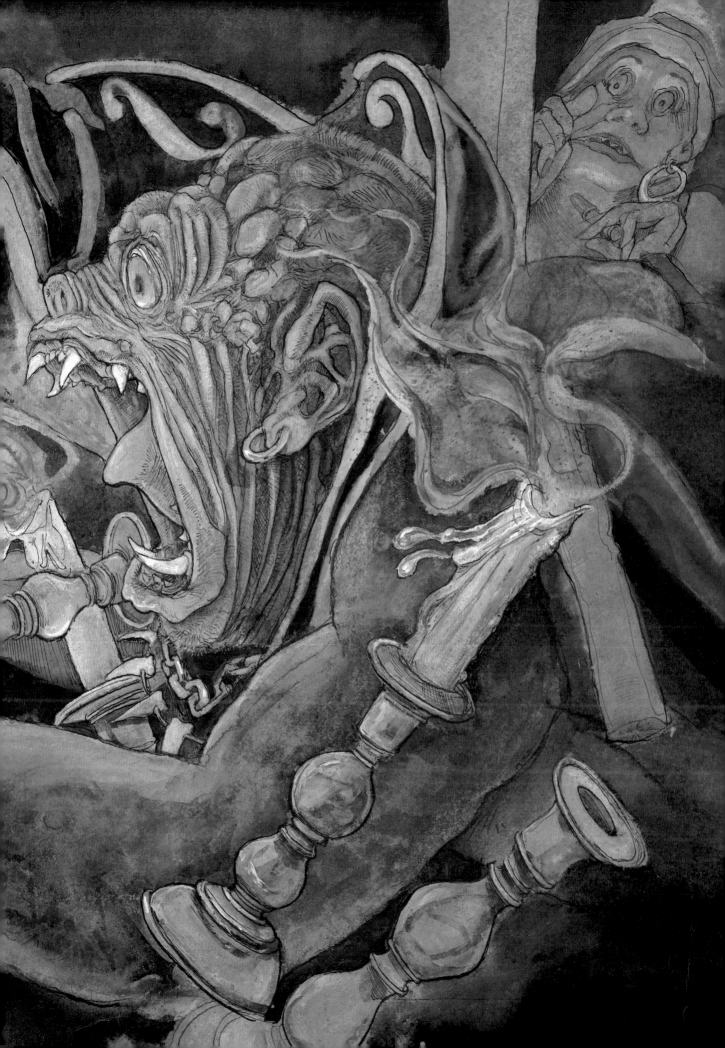

Jack ran as fast as he could and the ogre came rushing after.

When the ogre saw Jack climbing down for dear life, he swung himself onto the beanstalk, which shook with his weight. Down climbed Jack, and after him climbed the ogre. Jack called out, "Mother! Mother! Bring me an ax."

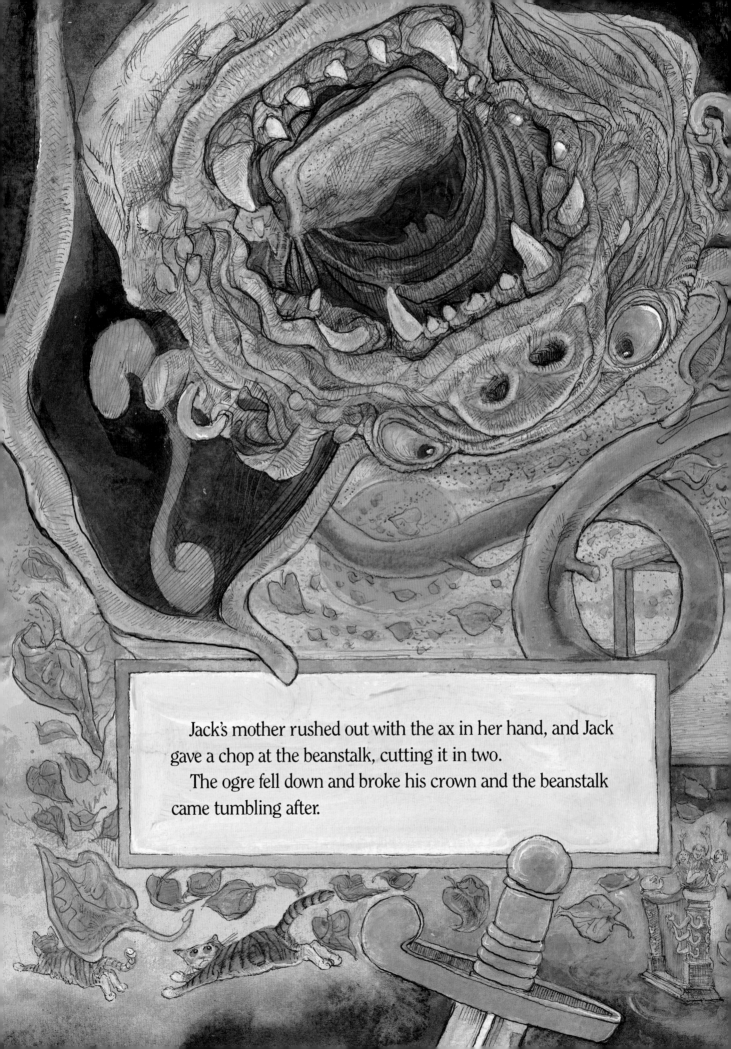

Jack's mother rushed out with the ax in her hand, and Jack gave a chop at the beanstalk, cutting it in two.

The ogre fell down and broke his crown and the beanstalk came tumbling after.

What with showing the golden harp and selling the golden eggs, Jack and his mother became very rich, and Jack married a great princess and they all lived happily ever after.